MASK

THE PLUNDER OF GLOW-WORM GROTTO

Welcome to the world of
**MASK –
MOBILE ARMOURED STRIKE
KOMMAND**

Imagine a world where there is more
to reality than meets the eye. Where
illusion and deception team up with
man and machine to create a world of
sophisticated vehicles and weaponry,
manned by agents and counter-agents.

The Plunder of Glow-worm Grotto
The MASK mission: to protect the
sacred Maori treasure from plunder by
VENOM. Scott Trakker and his robot
companion T-Bob help MASK in a
perilous situation.

The sixth thrilling **MASK** adventure.

MATT TRAKKER – SPECTRUM

MATT TRAKKER – ULTRA FLASH

HONDO MACLEAN – BLASTER

BRAD TURNER – HOCUS POCUS

BUDDIE HAWKES – PENETRATOR

DUSTY HAYES – BACKLASH

BRUCE SATO – LIFTER

ALEX SECTOR – JACKRABBIT

CLIFF DAGGER – THE TORCH

SLY RAX – STILETTO

MILES MAYHEM – VIPER

MASK

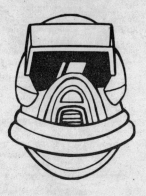

THE PLUNDER OF GLOW-WORM GROTTO

novelisation by
Kenneth Harper

Illustrated by Bruce Hogarth

KNIGHT BOOKS
Hodder and Stoughton

Text copyright © Kenneth
Harper 1987
Illustrations copyright © Bruce
Hogarth 1987

First published in Great Britain
by Knight Books 1987

Mask TM and the associated
trade marks are the property of
Kenner Parker Toys Inc. (KPT)
1987

Printed and bound in Great
Britain for Hodder and
Stoughton Paperbacks, a
division of Hodder and
Stoughton Limited, Mill Road,
Dunton Green, Sevenoaks, Kent
(Editorial Office: 47 Bedford
Square, London WC1B 3DP) by
Cox & Wyman Limited, Cardiff
Road, Reading, Berks.
Photoset by Rowland
Phototypesetting Limited,
Bury St Edmunds, Suffolk.

British Library C.I.P.

Harper, Kenneth, 1940
    The plunder of Glow-worm
    Grotto. – (MASK; 6).
    Rn: Keith Miles   I. Title
    II. Hogarth, Bruce   III. Series
    823'914[J]   PZ7

    ISBN 0-340-41535-5

MASK

ONE

The Maori village was situated in a remote area on North Island. Log cabins had been built in a circle then surrounded by a high timber fence. Beyond that fence were several hot water geysers from which steam was curling upwards into the night sky. In the background, rising above it all in lone splendour, was an extinct volcano.

There was a primitive beauty to the whole scene.

'What a place!' murmured Julio Lopez.

'You like?' asked Chief Kaitaia.

'Yeah – it's great!'

Julio gazed around the central yard which was illumined by large torches. In the glowing firelight, he

admired the ornate carvings that stood on every side. They were very striking.

Boom-butty-boom-butty-boom-butty-boom!

The stillness of the night was shattered by the pounding rhythm. Hands beat down on drums and stout sticks were used to hit hollow logs. The sound echoed across the countryside.

All the warriors of the tribe gathered in formation and began to dance to the powerful rhythm. They were big, strong, proud, fierce-looking men. They wore simple loincloths, armbands and headbands. Each man wore a necklace of seed pods and shells. They all carried a spear in one hand and a fern bough in the other. Their dark bodies were covered in tattoos and their faces were painted with bright colours.

Boom-butty-boom-butty-boom-butty-boom!

Their bare feet kicked up a small cloud of dust.

Julio Lopez watched with interest. He sat on the ground beside the Maori chief. In front of them was a low wooden table that was loaded with fish, lamb, fruit and drink. Three other places had been set at the table but they were empty.

Chief Kaitaia was a tall, thin, imposing figure. He wore a magnificent feathered cape and an elaborate head-dress. Like his warriors, his face was painted with dramatic effect. Around his neck was a glistening pearl and shell necklace.

Boom-butty-boom-butty-boom-butty-boom!

'These guys can really dance,' said Julio.

'This is the traditional Maori challenge,' explained the chief. 'All visitors are greeted this way.'

'Oh, I see.'

'Take this.'

Chief Kaitaia offered him a bough of fern.

'Why?' asked Julio.

'Take the fern and clasp it to your chest,' said the chief. 'If you are a friend.'

'Well, I'm definitely a *friend*.'

He accepted the fern and touched it to his chest near his heart. The chief was pleased. A thought struck Julio.

'What happens to enemies?'

'In the old days, the Maori warriors cut off heads to keep as trophies.'

'Oh!' gasped Julio.

Chief Kaitaia let out a rumbling laugh.

'We are civilized people now. Your head is safe.'

Julio smiled and fingered his neck.

'I'm glad to hear it,' he said. 'I've grown rather attached to mine.'

'It is a good head,' agreed his host.

Chief Kaitaia rose to his feet and signalled with his hand. The drumming stopped at once and the warriors abandoned their dance. They stood in ranks and listened in respectful silence as their leader addressed them.

'My friends, tonight we have great cause to celebrate . . .'

The Maori warriors nodded in unison.

'The Matt Trakker Foundation will help us to preserve our culture,' added the chief.

He gestured to Julio who stood up and gave a broad grin, holding the fern across his chest to show that he was a friend.

Chief Kaitaia introduced their guest.

'This is their representative, Julio Lopez. He will join us in our feast tonight.'

'Thank you, Chief Kaitaia.'

The Maori leader glanced at the empty places at the table.

'I had hoped to welcome Mr Trakker himself,' he said.

'Yes,' replied Julio. 'Matt and his son wanted to be here tonight but they must have been delayed. They're flying in from Rotorua.' His grin appeared again. 'Guess their arms got tired, huh?'

Dead silence greeted his remark. Blank faces stared at him. Chief Kaitaia was as grim and impassive as the rest of them.

'Uh . . . just a little joke, folks,' explained Julio.

The chief's eyebrows shot up with sudden interest.

'Oh!' he said. 'That was a joke?'

'Yeah. A small one.'

'So it was funny?'

'Well . . . sort of, Chief.'

The Maori leader threw back his head and burst out laughing. Julio was completely taken by surprise. Chief Kaitaia turned to his warriors and waved a hand. They joined in the raucous laughter.

11

Within a few seconds, they were positively shaking with mirth.

Julio Lopez was bemused by it all.

'It wasn't *that* funny,' he said to himself.

Chief Kaitaia stopped abruptly.

'Joke finished!' he announced.

The laughter ceased at once and the warriors stood still.

'You are an honoured guest,' said the chief to Julio. 'We are delighted that someone is here to represent the Matt Trakker Foundation. The gift to us is very generous.'

'That's Matt for you,' replied Julio.

Matt Trakker was a multi-millionaire with a special interest in the preservation of ancient cultures. His well-known generosity had turned him into a celebrated philanthropist and he had been especially keen to help the Maoris.

But there was much more to Matt Trakker than his money. He was the founder and the controlling force behind MASK – the Mobile Armoured Strike Kommand which had pledged itself to fight against evil in all its forms and which used its high technology weaponry in that eternal struggle.

Julio Lopez was one of the highly-trained MASK agents. He enjoyed being on a peaceful mission for once.

'I like New Zealand,' he said.

'So do we,' replied his host. 'North Island is our home.'

'It's fantastic! Like being in paradise. There's no sign of VENOM at all.'

'VENOM?'

'A nasty bunch, Chief,' explained Julio. '*They* wouldn't hold a fern across their chest. There's nothing friendly about VENOM. Just be glad that it's *me* who's here and not them.'

'We are glad,' added Kaitaia. 'We show you.'

Turning on his heel, the Maori leader strode to the centre of the yard and flung off his cape in dramatic style. By the light of the flickering torches, Julio could see that the chief's body was covered in a raised geometrical tattoo. On his back was a particularly complex design.

Chief Kaitaia held up both hands.

'The warriors' dance will now start.'

Drums began to beat once more and the hollow logs were struck even harder. Everyone danced in time to the strong rhythm.

Boom-butty-boom-butty-boom-butty-boom!

Julio Lopez was mesmerized by it all.

'Wow! What a cabaret!'

Staying strictly in step, the warriors moved from side to side and then forward and backwards. It was a vigorous dance and they put all their energy into it. When they gestured with their spears in a warlike fashion, Julio was relieved that he was there as a friend. He hated the idea of being in the position of an enemy to the Maori tribe.

'Yaaaaaaow!'

He put his hand over his mouth to stifle the yawn that had just escaped him. Julio could not understand it. A second ago he was wide awake. Now he was becoming quite sleepy.

'What's wrong with me?' he asked. 'Wake up, Julio!'

He tried to jerk himself awake again so that he could concentrate on the dance that was being performed in his honour. It would be ill-mannered of him to nod off.

'Yaaaaaaow!'

A second yawn suddenly oozed out of him.

'Hey, what's happening!' he explained.

When he looked at Chief Kaitaia, he saw the Maori leader split into three. It was the same with the other warriors. They all seemed to have multiplied and were jumping about wildly. Julio rubbed his eyes and stared again.

The light from the torches was much brighter now and an acrid smoke was given off. In the glare of the flames, Julio saw something that was even more remarkable.

Boom-butty-boom-butty . . .

The drumming tailed off altogether.

The warriors stopped dancing and began to sway.

Crash!

First, one of them fell to the ground in a heap and then another. More soon followed. Wherever Julio looked, the Maoris seemed to be dropping as if in a deep sleep. The yard was soon littered with prostrate bodies.

Chief Kaitaia was the last to go. He tried to say

something to his guest but weariness overcame him and down he went.

Crash!

Julio did his best to fight off his own fatigue.

'Maybe if I walk around a bit . . .'

When he attempted to move, however, he only wobbled. His legs had turned to jelly and would not support him. He stared at the torch which was burning near him. Its flame had changed colour now and it was giving off an even more insidious aroma.

'That isn't lamp-oil!' he decided. 'It's . . . sleeping gas!'

He lurched away from the torch.

'I've got to get out of . . .'

But the words died on his lips. Like everyone else in the village, Julio Lopez lapsed into a deep and lasting slumber. He lay face down on the ground and was lost to the world.

He did not see the three shadows that soon moved across the earth. And he did not hear the dark and malicious laughter that rang through the village.

Evil was at hand.

TWO

Thunder Hawk shot through the air at supersonic speed. Matt Trakker was at the controls of the MASK vehicle which had converted to jet mode. Sitting beside the pilot was his adopted son, Scott, a bright, enquiring and often mischievous boy with a ready grin. Also aboard was T-Bob, the comical robot who was Scott's constant companion.

As Matt stared through the front window, the signs were ominous. He shook his head and sighed.

'We've got a storm coming,' he warned.

'Can't we avoid it, Dad?' asked Scott.

'I hate stormy weather,' moaned T-Bob, holding his midriff. 'It makes me feel seasick.'

'How can you feel seasick in a plane?' said Scott with

a giggle. 'Do you feel air-sick when you're on a ship?'

'You know what I mean,' retorted the robot. 'It's all that being thrown around.'

'We're in for a bit of that, I'm afraid,' added Matt.

The sky ahead was black and thick clouds were swirling angrily. A ferocious wind was already starting to buffet Thunder Hawk. The storm broke with spontaneous fury.

Rumble-rumble-rumble-rumble!

Shizoo!

Thunder rolled and forked lightning blazed.

The MASK vehicle was knocked about as if being slapped by giant hands. Matt did his best to steady the machine but the elements were too powerful. Thunder Hawk shook and rattled.

T-Bob closed his eyes and held on to his seat.

'Ohhhhh!' he wailed.

'This is fun!' yelled Scott. 'Just like being on a switchback at Disneyland. Up we go, then – dooooooown!'

Shizoo!

More lightning flashed across the heavens.

'This electric storm is affecting the instruments,' noted Matt, flicking switches on his console. 'I can't get proper readings.'

'Who wants to *read* at a time like this?' howled T-Bob.

'This is serious,' said Matt. 'I don't know where we're going. The computer is not responding.'

'I'll tell you where we're going, Dad,' replied Scott

happily, as the vehicle was caught by another gust. 'We're going uuuuuuup and then we're going doooooown!'

'Don't keep saying that!' cried T-Bob.

'We're being blown right off course,' observed Matt. 'Julio is going to have to dine without us. We're not going to make it to the village for quite some while.'

He continued to adjust the controls. Thunder Hawk was equipped with all the latest technological gadgets but its size was against it. It stood no chance against the surging wind which carried it here, there and everywhere.

The storm raged for hours. When it finally blew itself out, it had taken Thunder Hawk way out to sea. They were flying across the great expanse of the Pacific Ocean.

'I'm glad *that's* over,' said Matt. 'It was worse than being ambushed by VENOM.'

'My tummy will never be the same again!' complained the robot, holding his midriff again.

'Don't be silly, T-Bob,' said Scott with a laugh. 'You don't have a tummy.'

'I don't *now*,' rejoined his friend. 'I lost it back there when we went uuuuuuup and then doooooown!'

Matt now had control of Thunder Hawk once more and was able to set them back on course. Though the vehicle rocketed across the night sky, there was no way that they could make up the lost time. They were going to be very late for the party.

Scott began to feel hungry. He turned to Matt.

'I hope they won't have eaten all the food, Dad.'

'Don't worry, son. According to Julio, these Maori celebrations go on for days. We won't have missed everything.'

'Good! I'm starving!'

'I couldn't eat a thing!' sighed T-Bob.

'Robots don't eat,' reminded Scott.

'And it's just as well,' added his little companion.

Dawn was breaking as they flew in over North Island and headed towards the Maori village. Matt brought Thunder Hawk in low so that they could get a close look at the terrain before landing.

Set amid the green hills of New Zealand were the steaming geysers and the old volcano. Scott pointed a finger at them.

'Gee, Dad!' he exclaimed. 'Look at those geysers and that huge crater. Is it going to erupt?'

'No,' said Matt. 'It's extinct. That's the Waimangu Thermal Valley. It's filled with geysers that the natives tap into for heat and cooking.'

'Look at all that steam rising up!' added the boy.

T-Bob lay back in his seat and groaned.

'I don't want to look at anything. I need my beauty sleep. That storm took all the steam out of me.'

The robot closed his eyes and began to doze off.

His slumber was short-lived. Thunder Hawk banked, then swept down to land on a level stretch of ground. As its wheels touched down, it converted back to sports-car mode. Its gull-like wings were folded away and its tail-fin was retracted.

As they drove towards the village, the sun was starting to rise. Matt took the car around the timber fence and in through the open gateway. When Thunder Hawk came to a halt, its three passengers gazed around in astonishment.

Everybody was still fast asleep on the ground.

'Some party!' decided Scott. 'They've all grabbed some shuteye.'

'I can't wait to join them,' said T-Bob with a yawn.

'Did they have too much to drink, Dad?' asked the boy.

'I don't think so,' replied Matt, studying the prone bodies with mild alarm. 'Something funny is going on here. This is no slumber party.'

'What a pity!' sighed T-Bob.

The MASK leader jumped out of Thunder Hawk.

'Come on. Let's investigate.'

They got out and followed him across the yard, stepping over the Maoris as they did so. Matt spotted what he was after.

'Julio – there he is!'

The three of them ran across to the unconscious figure of the MASK agent who was still lying face down. Matt took him by the shoulders and gave him a gentle shake.

'Hey! Wake up, old buddy!'

'What . . .?' murmured Julio, drowsily.

He turned over and blinked in the early morning sun. He could not at first make out the face of the man who was holding him. Very slowly, the blurred image came into sharper focus.

Julio managed a tired smile of gratitude.

'Matt? Scotty?'

'Don't forget *me*,' said T-Bob, coming forward.

'I'm so groggy,' admitted Julio, holding his head.

'What happened?' asked Matt.

'I wish I knew,' replied the MASK agent.

He sat up and shook his head to clear it more thoroughly. When he saw the Maori warriors still asleep all around him, he began to piece together a memory of events.

'Last night,' he recalled. 'The celebration . . . dancing . . . the torches . . . that strange smell . . .'

'What smell?' pressed Matt.

'The one that did the damage,' explained Julio. 'It had to be – sleeping gas! Somebody filled the torches with sleeping gas.'

'Maybe it was your old flame,' suggested T-Bob.

'That's a rotten joke!' complained Scott.

The robot chuckled and showed that he could do worse.

'I'll bet that party was a real gas!'

Matt, Julio and Scott all groaned this time.

Other groans were now heard but not in response to T-Bob's feeble sense of humour. They came from the Maori warriors who were stirring from their sleep. One by one, they came awake and struggled to stand up. All of them were totally mystified.

'Aaaagh!'

The warriors noticed something that made them shout. They ran to the centre of the yard and crowded around with concern. Matt, Scott and T-Bob had no idea what was going on.

Julio scrambled to his feet and explained it all.

'It's Chief Kaitaia,' he said. 'Come!'

The four of them raced over to join the crowd. They were just in time to see the Maori chief coming slowly out of his sleep. What had alarmed the warriors was the fact that their leader's body was completely covered in some kind of blue paint.

Chief Kaitaia looked at the paint in surprise.

'What is this?'

'I'm not sure,' said T-Bob. 'Maybe you've got the blues.'

'I was sent to sleep,' recalled the chief. 'We all were.'

One of his warriors came running up to make a report.

'I have searched the village,' he announced. 'Nothing is harmed. Nothing has been stolen.'

'The village has not been touched,' added Julio.

'Except for me,' Chief Kaitaia pointed out.

'Looks like you had a brush with someone,' noted T-Bob.

He laughed merrily at his own joke but nobody else did.

'Why would they paint me but not steal anything?' asked the Maori leader, his hand going to his throat. 'They did not even take my pearl necklace.'

Matt and Julio discussed what had happened but

they could throw no light on the strange events. It was Scott who came to their aid. He wandered off to the edge of the village and spotted something that turned out to be a vital clue. Instinct made him yell out.

'Dad! Julio! Quick – over here!'

'Why?' called Matt.

'Look what I've found.'

They all hurried across to Scott and stood in a circle around him. He was kneeling on the ground beside two long parallel marks. They were quite deep and a few metres apart. Julio Lopez recognized them at once as the marks of a helicopter.

'Strut marks,' he decided. 'Familiar, Matt?'

'Yes,' agreed his leader. 'Switchblade.'

'What is this Switchblade?' asked Chief Kaitaia.

'A helicopter,' said Matt. 'It belongs to a very twisted and dangerous man called Miles Mayhem. The brain behind VENOM!' He rubbed his chin thoughtfully. 'So – *he* is our party gate-crasher!'

'But why would VENOM want to paint the town?' wondered Julio. 'Or should I say – the chief?'

Matt smiled for a moment, then became deadly serious.

'I don't know yet but you can bet that Mayhem didn't come all this way to practise his brush strokes. He's up to something.'

'What is it?' said Chief Kaitaia.

'I wish I knew,' answered Matt. 'The first thing we must do is to analyse that paint they covered you in, Chief. That might give us a vital lead.'

'I'll take a sample of the paint,' added Julio, responding with the usual efficiency of a MASK agent. 'Then I'll check it out.'

'Meanwhile, I'll get help,' asserted Matt.

'*We* can help,' offered Chief Kaitaia.

'VENOM is a lethal enemy,' warned Matt.

'We can be lethal as well,' promised the Maori leader.

He gave the signal to his men who brandished their spears and set up a warlike chant. It was an impressive sight. They were brave warriors who would be fearless in battle but Matt knew that they would be useless against VENOM. Spears and chants were no match for the sophisticated weaponry that Miles Mayhem and his cohorts had at their disposal.

Matt Trakker, however, had to be tactful. He did not want to offend the chief by spurning his offer too abruptly.

'Thanks for the suggestion,' he said to the Maori leader. 'Hold your men in reserve in case we need them. Though somehow I don't think that we will.'

'Why not?' demanded Chief Kaitaia.

'Because this is a job with our name on it.'

'Name?'

'MASK!'

Matt wasted no more time.

He sprang into action.

THREE

Thunder Hawk was parked near Chief Kaitaia's cabin, which was larger and more elaborate than the other dwellings. But Matt Trakker had no time to admire the timber structure with its curious carvings. He jumped straight into Thunder Hawk and punched a button on the console. His voice was urgent.

'Satellite link to MASK computer,' he ordered. 'Select best agents for special mission in North Island, New Zealand. Julio Lopez already pre-selected.'

The machine whirred and bleeped for a few seconds. The image on the screen scrambled then cleared. Bruce Sato's face came up on the screen along with a computer graphic representation of his MASK combat vehicle.

The computer's voice was calm, collected and female.

'Recommended personnel: Bruce Sato, mechanical engineer and design specialist. Thunder Hawk co-pilot. Lifter mask could be essential on this assignment.'

'Approved,' said Matt.

Another face and another vehicle came up on the screen.

'Dusty Hayes,' continued the female voice. 'All-terrain specialist. Vehicle code name: Gator.'

'Approved.'

The computer image scrambled once more and the lovely face of Gloria Baker came into view. The voice spoke on.

'Gloria Baker, champion racing car driver, black belt in karate. Vehicle code name: Shark.'

Matt nodded with enthusiasm. The voice carried on.

'Agents Hayes and Baker command amphibious vehicles valuable in exploration of island waterways. Selection complete.'

'Personnel approved!' announced Matt. 'Assemble Mobile Armoured Strike Kommand!'

As he gave the order, Matt Trakker pressed a button on his watch. The word MASK flashed on a liquid-crystal display.

The wristwatch sent its signal to the three agents who had been chosen. Bruce Sato, a brilliant engineer, was in his workshop to test out his latest toy. It was a small mechanical dragon which he had designed to work by remote control. He flicked a switch to set the little creature in motion and the dragon moved across the table, belching out flames through its mouth.

Bruce then received the signal on his watch and abandoned his experiment. While he dashed out through the door, his dragon kept on walking towards the open window. Outside in the garden, a tiny dog was being menaced by a big black one. The dragon tripped over the window sill, fell to the ground, rolled over and stood up so that it was now protecting the weaker animal. It opened its steel jaws and shot a flame into the surprised face of the big dog.

Dusty Hayes, meanwhile, was taking part in a rodeo. Wearing his stetson and whooping with delight, he sat astride a bucking bronco that was trying to hurl him off. With great encouragement from his friends, Dusty was hanging on and could not be unsaddled.

Then his watch flashed and he obeyed the call by reflex. The next time that the bronco bucked, the rider simply let go and sailed off through the air. Nobody could understand it, least of all the bronco itself. It stared after the departing cowboy with its mouth wide open.

Gloria Baker got her summons while she was dancing at a disco club with her date. Her watch buzzed and she forgot all about the throbbing music and the pleasant young man opposite her. When he twirled her around, she went spinning off across the room and her date found himself dancing with one of the waitresses instead.

Bruce Sato. Dusty Hayes. Gloria Baker.

Highly-trained agents on a special assignment.

They converged on Boulder Hill Gas Station, beneath which MASK headquarters was cunningly hidden. In no time at all, the three of them had boarded their transport and were flying at top speed across the Pacific Ocean.

Mobile Armoured Strike Kommand was on its way!

Back on North Island, Julio Lopez was having some difficulty in analysing the blue paint. Watched by Matt, Scott and T-Bob, he worked at a table in Chief Kaitaia's log cabin. From his medical bag, Julio took various phials of coloured liquid. He used the chemical to test for a reaction from the paint.

'One thing,' he concluded. 'We know the paint's not poisonous or drugged.'

'Is it magnetic, by any chance?' asked Matt.

'No.' Julio reached a decision. 'I'd feel safer if we ran it through the computer.'

'Lead the way,' suggested Matt.

As the two men headed towards Thunder Hawk again, Scott and T-Bob slipped away. They were going to nose around the village for their own clues.

The boy took the robot aside and whispered to him.

'What do you think that blue stuff is?'

'The latest Maori fashion,' said T-Bob.

'Fashion?'

'Yes – a coat of paint. Get it? A *coat* . . .'

Scott wished that he had never bothered to ask.

Matt and Julio were getting a more sensible answer inside Thunder Hawk. Chemical formulae and molecular patterns flashed up on the screen as the paint was analysed.

The female voice then detailed the findings.

'Blue paint identified. Commonly used by cartographers on topographical maps to designate spatial relationships.'

'I don't get it,' admitted Julio.

'Nor me,' confessed Matt. 'Why would Mayhem want to cover Chief Kaitaia with map-maker's ink?'

'To give him some *relief*?'

Matt grimaced at the pun which was worthy of T-Bob. Then he thought again and looked back at the computer screen.

'Of course, Julio!' he said. 'A relief map! You're right!'

'Am I?'

'Let's take another look at those tattoos again.'

They left Thunder Hawk and sought out Chief Kaitaia. He was only too glad to help. Matt and Julio examined his back with growing fascination. A network of dark blue, raised lines covered his skin.

'This could be it,' said Matt, scrutinizing the pattern.

'But all Maori warriors have tattoos,' argued Chief Kaitaia. 'What is so unusual about mine?'

'It's different from the others,' explained Matt.

37

'Yes,' added Julio. *'They're* not covered with blue ink.'

'That's not all,' continued Matt, touching the chief's back. 'Feel this scar here, Julio.'

The MASK agent traced the line on the Maori's back with his finger. There seemed to be a small ridge in the flesh.

'It's raised,' he said. 'Like a . . .'

Matt Trakker supplied the words for him.

'Like a relief map!'

The two men exchanged a knowing look. It was no random tattoo on the chief's back. It was a contour map which obviously had enormous significance if it could attract the attention of Miles Mayhem and his henchmen.

Scott once again provided a vital clue.

'Dad!' he shouted. 'Look what T-Bob and I found!'

The boy and the robot came running across with some pieces of paper that they had retrieved from the ground. The paper was covered with ink that had been badly smeared.

Matt realized what must have happened.

'These are imprints of that map on the chief's back,' he said. 'Only they got smudged. VENOM must have tried several times before they got it right. And they wouldn't go to such trouble unless it was worth their while.' He showed the piece of paper to the Maori leader. 'Does this map mean anything to you?'

'No,' admitted Chief Kaitaia. 'I don't know what it is or why it should have been tattooed on my back.'

Matt Trakker's brow was furrowed with anxiety.

'I don't like this,' he said frankly. 'There are too many unanswered questions. We don't know what VENOM is after or why.'

'Or where they'll strike next,' observed Julio.

Matt glanced with concern at Scott and T-Bob then he turned to ask a favour of Chief Kaitaia.

'As you can see, I have my family with me. Until we can find out what's going on, Chief, I'd feel better if they were in a safe place.'

'Of course,' replied the Maori leader. 'There is Waitomo Grotto. It is sacred to our people. And my uncle is the priest who guards it. The little ones will be safe there.'

Scott Trakker snorted in disgust.

'Little ones! I like that!'

Chief Kaitaia signalled to a guard who went off towards a cabin on the other side of the square. A guide was clearly being sent for and the idea upset Scott.

'Why do we have to miss out on all the fun, Dad?'

'Danger is not fun,' warned Matt.

'I agree,' said T-Bob. 'We'll be much better off in this sacred grotto. It'll give us a chance to catch up on some sleep.'

'I can't sleep when there's action going on,' protested Scott. 'Let me stay with you in Thunder Hawk, Dad.'

'Not this time, son.'

'You will like it in the Waitomo Grotto,' promised

Chief Kaitaia with a smile. 'Wait till you meet your guide.'

'I don't want to be packed off,' continued Scott.

'Well, I do,' said T-Bob firmly. 'When VENOM is around, I want to get right off the map.'

'Listen to T-Bob for once,' advised Matt. 'He's talking sense. Besides, you might actually enjoy seeing this sacred place.'

'Not a chance!' asserted the boy.

'Are you sure?' teased Chief Kaitaia.

'Yeah,' insisted Scott.

'Tell that to your guide,' suggested the Maori.

'I don't want any guide,' Scott argued. 'Nothing could possibly make me want to go to this crummy grotto with some dumb . . .'

The words died on his lips and his eyes widened.

Scott Trakker changed his mind in an instant.

He had just caught sight of his guide.

She was beautiful.

FOUR

Scott Trakker stood there with his mouth agape. The
girl who was walking towards him was about his own
age. She had a round, sunny face that was set off by a
dazzling smile and she wore a short, striped reed skirt
with a halter top. The girl was a vision of loveliness.
He was hypnotized.

'Hello,' she said brightly.

'Uh . . . oh . . . yeah . . . hi,' he replied.

'My name is Te Kaha.'

'I'm S-s-s-s-scott T-t-t-t-trakker,' he stuttered.

'Pleased to meet you.'

Te Kaha leaned forward to give him a traditional
Polynesian greeting. She brushed her nose very gently

against his. Scott was at once delighted and embarrassed. His cheeks flushed.

The girl took a flower from her hair and gave it to him.

'Say it with flowers,' mocked T-Bob, giggling.

Scott blushed even more deeply.

Chief Kaitaia traded a glance with Matt Trakker. They both grinned. It was obvious that the boy would make no more protests about having to go off with a guide.

'It is a beautiful journey to Waitomo,' said Te Kaha.

'I can't wait!' responded Scott.

'Perhaps my grandfather will take us through the caves. They are lit only by glow-worms.'

'Sounds *glow*-rious to me,' remarked T-Bob.

Scott did not even hear the pun. His eyes were locked on Te Kaha. She was the prettiest girl he had ever seen. His nose was still tingling from contact with her.

Te Kaha extended her greeting to T-Bob as well, but with a very different result. When she leaned forward to rub her nose gently against him, the robot let out a series of mechanical noises and jumped backwards in alarm.

'Hey, watch it!' he protested.

'Don't get your nose out of joint, T-Bob,' teased Matt. 'Our young friend here is taking you to the grotto for your own protection.'

'In that case,' said the robot, 'we'd better get going.'

Scott saw a chance to take charge in order to impress Te Kaha. He stepped up to the robot and snapped an order.

'Scooter mode, T-Bob.'

'What's that?' asked the girl.

'I'll show you,' answered Scott.

He was looking at her as he spoke and his attention was distracted from T-Bob, who was slow in converting to scooter mode. When Scott went to sit down, therefore, he discovered that there was no seat ready for him and he fell to the ground with a thud. Te Kaha giggled and the boy turned red.

'Hurry up, T-Bob!' he hissed angrily.

'Don't rush me, don't rush me!'

The robot's wheels and seat came into view and the scooter was ready. Scott climbed on to the seat and moved forward so that Te Kaha could get on behind him.

'You'll have to hold on tight,' warned Matt.

The girl wrapped her arms around Scott who loved it. The adults looked on with amusement. T-Bob waited patiently for his next command.

'Let's move it!' ordered Scott.

The scooter roared into life and pulled away. With Te Kaha clinging to him, Scott headed for the gateway. His face beamed.

Matt Trakker chuckled then called after him.

'We should be there to pick you up fairly soon.'

'No rush!' replied the boy. 'I'm in good hands.'

They swept out through the gateway in a cloud of dust.

The adults burst into laughter.

The MASK transport had made good time on its hectic journey across the vast Pacific. Bruce Sato, Dusty Hayes and Gloria Baker sat in a row at the console. All three were now in combat uniforms. The transport zoomed in over North Island and began its descent.

Bruce Sato flicked a switch and made radio contact.

'Hello, Kemosabe!' he said into the microphone.

Matt Trakker's voice answered from inside Thunder Hawk.

'Hey, honourable sidekick!' he said. 'It's about time that you got here.'

Bruce Sato glanced through the window at the terrain below, then he confided his problem to Matt.

'These trees and hills are gonna make Firefly landing a little difficult. Any suggestions?'

'Yes,' replied Matt. 'I spotted some flat land near that volcano when I was coming in. You could try that.'

'Thanks for the tip.'

Another voice came over the intercom. It was Julio Lopez.

'Be careful where you set my buggy down, Bruce. There's still geyser activity in that area.'

Bruce Sato had already made a note of that fact.

'It's a risk we'll have to take, guys,' he argued. 'I can't land her on water . . . yet.'

'Okay, Bruce,' said Matt. 'Proceed with the landing but be on the alert for those geysers.'

'Will do, Matt,' came the reply. 'Besides, I've got Julio's fly-buggy to cushion my fall.'

'Don't you damage Firefly!' urged Julio. 'You be careful with my baby, do you hear?'

'I hear,' said Bruce. 'Over and out.'

He made his way to the cargo deck of the transport and got into the driving seat of Julio's combat vehicle. Firefly was an ordinary dune buggy to all outward appearances. When the cargo door opened, however, Bruce pressed a switch and the vehicle sprouted wings. With a surge of power, it took off and shot clear of the MASK transport.

Watching from below, Matt and Julio saw once again how Firefly had got its name. It looked very much like a larger version of the insect. Bruce brought it over the designated area then it started to descend.

Suddenly, a hot geyser erupted in a blast of boiling water directly in the path of the vehicle. Its pilot was caught unawares.

'Oh no!'

He swerved Firefly out of the way but met with more danger. Another geyser went off and its powerful jet of water hit one of the wings so hard that the craft went into a mid-air spin.

Bruce Sato fought desperately to regain control.

'Hang on in there!' encouraged Matt.

'Save Firefly!' urged Julio.

46

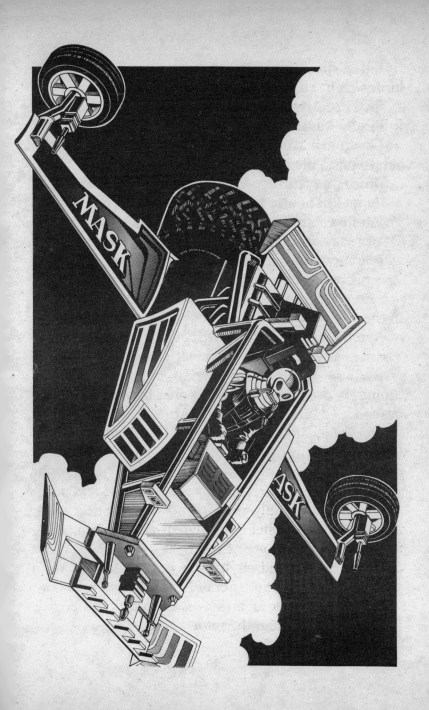

But the pilot was not sure that he could save himself or his craft. He was spinning uncontrollably now.

'I've been steam-cleaned. Now I'm in tumble-dry!'

Firefly was hurtling towards a mountainous wall of rock. Collision seemed unavoidable. It would be smashed to pieces.

Bruce saw the mountain racing towards him.

'Now I'm on my way to "permanent press"!'

Firefly was spinning towards certain doom.

'Mayday, Transport!' yelled Bruce. 'I'm a goner!'

But Dusty Hayes had other ideas. When he saw the terrible predicament that his friend was in, he pressed a button and his mask dropped automatically over his face.

'It ain't sayonara yet, pardner,' he promised, then he gave a command to his mask. 'Backlash – on!'

Backlash responded by sending out a shock wave that was accompanied by a sonic boom. The wave scored a direct hit on the mountain and the rock crumbled away in Firefly's path. It was able to fly on through to safety.

Once clear of immediate danger, Bruce Sato brought the craft under control. It stopped spinning and right-ed itself again.

'Eeyahoo, Bruce!' roared Dusty. 'Ride 'em, cow-boy!'

Bruce brought Firefly down until it landed on a patch of open ground. Its wings vanished as it con-verted back to a dune buggy. Everyone was relieved, no one more so than the pilot.

The transport itself was now brought into land. When the cargo door opened, Dusty and Gloria drove out in their respective combat vehicles, Gator and Shark.

Bruce Sato drove up in Firefly and screeched to a halt beside his two colleagues. He waved to Dusty.

'Thanks for bailing me out of that hot water.'

'Any time, Bruce,' said Dusty with a grin. 'I'm not ready to hang you out with the wash . . . yet!'

Gloria Baker rolled her eyes and groaned.

'No more jokes, fellas, okay? Matt's waiting.'

She gunned her motor and Shark took off in a swirl of dust. The other agents coughed and spluttered in her wake.

'No wonder they call me Dusty!' said Dusty.

He was covered in the stuff.

When they got to the village, Matt briefed his agents. They stood in a half-circle as they studied Chief Kaitaia's back. Gloria was impressed with its fine detail.

'Wow! That tattoo's got more lines than a road-map.'

'Good guess, Gloria,' congratulated Matt. 'We think it *is* a map. A family map.'

The chief turned around to face them.

'I remember when I was tattooed as a young man. The design was the same one as my father's . . . and the same as *his* father's.'

'It's the custom for all Maoris to have different

tattoos,' explained Julio. 'They pass them down through the generations.'

'Kind of like inheriting the family jewels?' said Dusty.

'In a manner of speaking, yes,' agreed Matt. 'But since it's on his back, the chief can't read *his* map.'

Bruce Sato had listened to it all with great care.

'Perhaps we would be wise to begin at the beginning.'

As usual, he was giving sound advice. Matt thanked him by patting him on the back. It was an intelligent plan.

'Bruce is right,' said Matt. 'We need the Maori who did the original tattoo. *He'd* know how to read the map.'

Chief Kaitaia identified the artist for them.

'The man you speak of is Paparoa, my uncle. He is a priest.'

'And the guardian of Glow-worm Grotto,' recalled Julio.

'If he's a guardian,' said Dusty, 'what's there to guard?'

'I only know that the caves are sacred,' replied Chief Kaitaia. 'A cultural heritage of our people.'

Matt Trakker became agitated all of a sudden.

'That's where we sent Scott and Te Kaha!'

Concern showed on every face as they realized the implications. The children were heading into serious danger.

'We'd better step on it,' urged Julio. 'Scott and the girl are probably there by now.'

'If it's sacred or valuable,' noted Gloria, 'then you-know-who will be there as well.'

'VENOM!' snapped Matt. 'Let's go!'

The MASK team raced off to their vehicles.

It was a dire emergency.

There was no time to lose.

FIVE

Glow-worm Grotto was located in an area of great natural beauty and charm. The River Waitomo flowed between verdant banks to a cavernous opening in a huge, craggy mountain. Trees, bushes and flowers abounded. Birds sang sweetly in the morning sunlight.

But something was disfiguring the scene. Three ugly and menacing vehicles were parked under the foliage.

Switchblade. Vampire. Piranha.

VENOM combat vehicles.

Miles Mayhem and two of his thugs, Sly Rax and Malloy, had come to the grotto on their latest malevolent quest and they were determined to get what they

sought. Wearing his hideous Viper mask, Mayhem had cornered Paparoa and forced him back against the limestone rock. He stood over the priest and threatened him.

Paparoa was a venerable old Maori who was dressed in a reed skirt, armbands, headband and necklace of shells and seed pods. Dangling from his necklace was a large conch.

Mayhem leaned in close and snarled angrily.

'Old man, show me the path to the secret cave!'

'I told you,' bleated Paparoa. 'There *is* no secret cave.'

'Then I'll make my own!' decided Mayhem before growling a command. 'Viper – on!'

A spurt of corrosive acid shot out from his mask and burned a large hole in the limestone rock just behind the priest. Paparoa cringed in fear. He was helpless against such power.

'I'll melt the whole grotto if I have to!' warned Mayhem.

'I *love* that mask, Mayhem!' said Rax with a snigger. 'Give us another demonstration.'

'No, no!' begged the priest.

Sly Rax drew himself up to his full height and adjusted the dark glasses that he always wore. He stared down at Paparoa.

'Let me have five minutes alone with this galoot,' he boasted. 'I'll soon have him talking treasure.'

'You *would* pick on an old man, Rax,' sneered Malloy.

'I suppose you'd be polite to him, marble-brain!'

Mayhem removed his mask and broke up the argument.

'Stop it, you two! Show him the map.'

Sly Rax pulled out a roll of paper that was covered with blue imprints made from Chief Kaitaia's tattoo. He thrust the paper directly under Paparoa's nose.

'According to our information,' he said, 'this map leads to a particular cavern.'

'Only problem is,' added Malloy. 'We can't read it.'

'That's not surprising,' retorted Rax. '*You* can't read your own name, Malloy.'

The little henchman shot Rax a hostile look.

'Read the map for me, old man!' ordered Mayhem. 'Now!'

Paparoa stared at him blankly as if he did not understand but the VENOM leader was not fooled. He could see that the priest was playing dumb. Mayhem took out a small transmitter and held it in front of Paparoa's face.

'Of course,' he threatened, 'I could just detonate that bomb I set back in your village. It would destroy the whole tribe.'

Mayhem's thumb moved closer to the detonator button.

'No, wait!' cried Paparoa in terror. 'I'll show you!'

'Get going then. Lead us to the secret grotto.'

Mayhem gave the old man a shove towards the entrance and Malloy moved off to his vehicle. Sly Rax took his leader aside and whispered a question to him.

'When did you have time to set a bomb?'

'I didn't,' said Mayhem. 'But *he* doesn't know that.'

Mayhem's thumb came down on the switch and a small flame appeared. It was not a transmitter at all but a cigarette lighter. Mayhem cackled, his eyebrows twitching and his great moustache bristling. Rax appreciated the joke that had been played on Paparoa.

'Let's get on with it!' ordered Mayhem.

Rax got into the sidecar of Piranha and converted it to submarine mode. It slipped into the river and floated into the cavern. Mayhem pushed Paparoa ahead of him along the path that ran along the riverside. Malloy followed on Vampire, his cycle-jet.

All three of them soon disappeared from sight in the darkness of the caves. They were on a treasure hunt.

Minutes later, Scott and Te Kaha arrived on the scooter and stopped outside a log cabin that had been built on stilts. T-Bob converted back again and his wheels vanished. The girl ran up steps that had been carved in the trunk of a tree and entered the cabin.

'Grandfather!' she called. 'Where are you, grandfather.'

'The cupboard is bare,' decided T-Bob.

Te Kaha reappeared and climbed down the steps.

'He's not here and I *so* wanted to show you the grotto.'

Scott pointed to a small canoe that was moored nearby.

'We could take that and paddle ourselves,' he said.

'Are you sure it's *safe*?' asked T-Bob anxiously.

'Oh, yes,' replied Te Kaha. 'My grandfather has taught me how to use it. And I know the way to Glow-worm Grotto.'

'All aboard!' shouted Scott.

He helped T-Bob into the canoe then Te Kaha pushed them off from the bank before jumping in beside them. The canoe was paddled towards the cavernous opening and the light of day was soon changed for the darkness of the interior.

'I miss home, where it's safe and *worm*,' wailed T-Bob.

Scott winced at the pun but kept on paddling. The blackness seemed to get even denser as they moved further on.

'I can't even see a hand in front of me – '

'*Face* it,' interrupted T-Bob, flicking on a light in his head. 'Without me, you'd be lost.'

'T-Bob,' said Te Kaha. 'The light must be off or the glow-worms won't shine for us.'

The robot shrugged and his light went out again.

'But it's too dark,' he complained. 'We might run into a wall or into . . .' There was a loud thud as they bumped into something solid. He was thrown back into the boat. 'A rock!'

'Shhh!' urged the girl. 'There must also be silence.'

'Pretty demanding bunch of worms,' murmured T-Bob.

'Isn't there any sound that doesn't scare them?'

asked Scott, staying very close to the lovely Te Kaha.

'Only one,' she said,' but grandfather has not taught me yet. It is a closely guarded secret. Now, everyone – quiet.'

They floated on in absolute silence.

The canoe entered a narrow passageway and cut through the water until it emerged into a large cavern. Suspended overhead were thousands of tiny, pulsing blue-green lights that bathed the whole place in a magic glow. The cavern was honeycombed with passages and festooned with colourful stalactites. Light shimmered on the water.

The effect was quite breathtaking.

'This is Glow-worm Grotto,' whispered Te Kaha.

'Wow!' murmured Scott. 'It's out of this world!'

'Heaven above and heaven below,' she said.

'So where are the worms?' asked T-Bob, mesmerized by it all.

'Those *are* the worms,' she explained. 'Up there.'

'Well, *glow*-ry be!'

'It's like some kind of fairyland,' noted Scott.

They feasted their eyes on the wonder of their surroundings but the treat did not last long. The lights suddenly went out and the grotto was plunged into darkness again.

'Hey!' said T-Bob. 'Who turned off the worms?'

'Something upset them,' replied Te Kaha.

'Well, they upset *me*, going off like that,' added the robot.

'Be quiet, T-Bob!' said Scott. 'I can hear something.'

'So can I,' agreed the girl. 'Voices. Further into the grotto. No wonder the glow-worms were disturbed.'

They strained their ears to try to identify the noises that were starting to echo through the cavern. The darkness made them fearful. Danger lurked ahead.

Miles Mayhem and his henchmen were not happy with the darkness either. They were blundering about in another cave. There was a dull thud.

'Aaaagh!' yelled Sly Rax.

'Shut up!' snarled Mayhem.

'But I can't see in this blackout. I keep running into things.'

'Serves you right, Rax,' sneered Malloy.

Then he himself collided with an outcrop of rock.

'Oooooh!'

Rax laughed and turned on the lights in Piranha's sidecar. Malloy was rubbing his arm gingerly. Mayhem snapped a command.

'Turn out that light!'

'But I don't like the dark,' complained Rax.

'The glow-worms won't glow with it on!'

Rax obeyed and the light went out. There was a pause.

'What are we gonna do?' demanded Malloy impatiently. 'Sit here in the pitch until the little crawlers wanna glow?'

'The priest will help us,' decided Mayhem.

'I have . . . forgotten the way,' said Paparoa.

'In that case, I'll have to melt this place down around

your ears.' Mayhem pretended to put his mask back on. 'Is that what you want me to do, old man?'

'No, please!'

The VENOM leader took out his cigarette lighter again.

'On the other hand, I could blow up your village. Maybe *that* would help you remember the way.'

'Stop!' implored Paparoa. 'I will do as you say.'

'Then let's have some action!'

'And some light!' said Rax.

The Maori priest heaved a sigh then reached for the conch shell that hung from his necklace. Putting it to his lips, he blew a high, sweet note. The glow-worms responded to his call at once. The roof of the cave began to pulse with light.

Mayhem and his men stared upwards. The glow-worms had arranged themselves in two parallel lines like the lights on either side of an airport runway. They were clearly directing the way.

'I feel like a 747 about to take off,' said Malloy.

'At least we can see where we're going now,' added Rax.

Mayhem gave Paparoa a shove in the back.

'Lead on, old man! Straight to the treasure!'

The canoe was heading towards the sound of the voices. When the cave ahead was bathed in a gentle glow, Te Kaha thought she caught a glimpse of her grandfather being bustled along.

'Hurry!' she urged. 'Paddle faster.'

65

'I'm doing my best,' said Scott, paddling hard.

'We must rescue grandfather.'

Te Kaha stood up in the canoe and craned her neck as she tried to look down the cave. It was a risky manoeuvre. The canoe brushed against a rock and wobbled dangerously. Before she knew what was happening, the girl was thrown into the water and carried off by the swift current.

'Help!' she cried.

Her life was now in peril.

SIX

Scott Trakker acted with speed and courage. Using the paddle to turn the canoe around, he worked strenuously to bring the little craft alongside Te Kaha. She was still out of his reach, however.

'Save me!' she shrieked.

'I'm coming!'

Scott dived into the water and swam across to her. He put one arm around her and used the other to battle against the current. Spitting out a mouthful of water, he called to T-Bob.

'Don't just sit there. Do something!'

'I can't swim!' reminded the robot.

'Get us out of here!'

T-Bob reached out an arm but they were too far

67

away. This did not defeat him. He simply program-
med both arms to telescope right out and got a firm
grip on the children. Slowly but surely, he pulled them
back aboard. His arms reduced to their normal size.

'Thanks, T-Bob,' said Scott.

'You saved our lives,' added Te Kaha.

She gave the robot a kiss and his metallic head
glowed.

The children were soaking wet but that did not
deflect them from their task. Paparoa was being held
by VENOM. The first priority was to try to rescue the
old man.

'I hope they don't hurt grandfather,' said Te Kaha.

'Mayhem will stop at nothing, I'm afraid,' replied
Scott. 'The sooner we get to them, the better.'

He turned the canoe around once more and paddled
in earnest.

'You're so strong and brave, Scott!' she said admir-
ingly.

'Thank you, Te Kaha.'

'I'll never forget the way you dived in after me. That
was so daring of you. I felt safe when you caught hold
of me.'

Scott smiled modestly and his cheeks burned. With
her dark hair plastered down by the water, Te Kaha
looked even more beautiful. He remembered her
greeting and his nose throbbed.

T-Bob brought his young friend back to reality.

'We won't stand much of a chance against them.'

'What are you on about, T-Bob?' asked the boy.

'VENOM. Even if we do find them, what can we do against those vicious criminals. We're not armed.'

'T-Bob is right,' admitted Te Kaha.

'We'll think of a way,' said Scott with bravado.

'I've thought of one,' added T-Bob. 'We must pray.'

'What for?' he asked.

'Your father and his agents. This is a job for MASK.'

In his heart, Scott Trakker agreed.

Only MASK could stand up against the might of VENOM.

The same thought had brought Matt Trakker and his colleagues to the entrance of the Waitomo Grotto. Parking their vehicles, they took a quick look around. There was no sign of the old priest or of the children. What they did see, however, was Switchblade. It was still parked under a tree.

'Well, we know that Mayhem's in there,' said Matt.

'And the kids as well, probably,' noted Julio. 'Look at those footprints on the bank. I'd know Scott's sneakers anywhere.'

'We must go in after them,' decided Matt.

'But we can't read the map,' warned Gloria. 'There's an intricate network of caves in there.'

'Yeah,' agreed Dusty. 'It's like a maze. We could be moseying around inside for hours without getting anywhere.'

'We'll manage somehow,' insisted Matt, anxious about the children's safety. 'Chief Kaitaia said the glow-worms would help us.'

70

Bruce Sato nodded and gave his sage advice.

'Trust in the tiny creatures and follow the light.'

'You heard him!' said Matt. 'Off we go.'

Mobile Armoured Strike Kommand did not hesitate.

Wearing their combat uniforms, they jumped into their respective vehicles. Dusty hopped back into Gator and converted it into floating mode so that he could enter the cavern by water. Gloria converted Shark to submarine mode so that she could follow.

Firefly remained in dune buggy mode with Julio at the controls. It took the path that ran alongside the river. Bringing up the rear was Thunder Hawk with Matt and Bruce inside.

They went into the cavern quickly and boldly.

MASK was stalking its mortal enemy once again.

Unaware of the arrival of Matt Trakker, VENOM had now got very close to their goal. They entered a large, circular cavern which had three exits. Mayhem consulted the map. The secret hiding place was marked on it but he could not see which of the three routes led to it.

The glow-worms formed a circle in the roof of the cavern. They had directed VENOM to the very heart of the grotto.

'This is it!' announced Mayhem.

'I don't see any treasure,' complained Rax.

'It's close!' promised the VENOM boss. 'I can smell it.'

71

'That's Malloy.'

'I don't smell!' shouted Malloy, sizing up to Rax.

'No,' said Rax. 'You *stink*!'

'Stop bickering, you two!' ordered Mayhem. 'Or I'll crack your stupid heads together. You're supposed to be on the same side.'

'Yeah,' grunted Rax.

'Sorry,' muttered Malloy.

Mayhem looked at the three exits that faced him.

'Which one leads to the secret cave, old man?' he demanded.

Paparoa cowered in terror as Mayhem raised a fist to hit him. But the blow never fell. Mayhem did not have to beat the truth out of the priest. The glow-worms told him what he wanted to know. They came together in a tight circle above the middle one of the three exits.

'That's the one!' said Mayhem.

'Those glow-worms came in real useful,' admitted Rax.

'More useful than you, anyway,' sneered Malloy.

'Listen to him! The laziest guy on the team.'

'Get in there, you idiots!' roared Mayhem.

He pushed his agents hard and they stumbled forward in front of him. When they reached the secret cave, Sly Rax and Malloy forgot all about their argument.

'Look at *that*!' said Rax with a grin.

'This beats everything!' agreed Malloy.

Mayhem's eyes gleamed with greed and malice.

'Didn't I tell you there'd be rich pickings?'

The secret cave was high and vaulted. Stalactites hung from the ceiling and stalagmites grew up from the floor to meet them. The whole place was illuminated by a brilliant shaft of light which came in through a hole in the roof of the cave and which set off the myriad colours.

What interested VENOM was the treasure – huge pearls that lay in giant oyster beds. One pearl alone would be worth millions.

'They're as big as basketballs!' noted Malloy with awe.

'Almost as big as your head,' quipped Rax.

'You're asking for it!' retorted his colleague.

'You couldn't scare a mouse!'

Miles Mayhem stepped between them and spoke angrily.

'I won't tell you two again! Cut the wisecracks, will you?' He surveyed the oyster beds once more. 'Beautiful! I should have brought a shopping cart!'

'Those pearls are terrific!' exclaimed Rax. 'If they had fingerholes, we could use them for bowling!'

'I'm not rolling them away from me!' asserted Malloy.

'Get busy!' snapped Mayhem.

'How many shall we take?' asked Rax.

'*All* of them,' insisted his leader.

The two agents walked off to the oyster beds to collect the massive pearls. Paparoa threw himself on Mayhem's mercy.

'Don't take them. *Please!*'

'Out of my way, old man!'

'But they're sacred!'

'We'll take good care of them.'

'You mustn't steal these Maori heirlooms.'

'Try stopping me!'

The priest dropped to his knees in supplication.

'Leave them alone, I beg you.'

'Save your breath!'

'But those pearls are all we have!'

'They're far more use to me than they are to the Maoris.'

'That's not true!' wailed Paparoa.

'Yes, it is,' argued Mayhem. 'You keep them hidden away here. I'll put them to proper use. This new wealth will help us in our fight against MASK. We'll earn enough money from those pearls to finance a whole new fleet of combat vehicles for VENOM. We'll be able to smash MASK once and for all. Once they're out of the way – the world is my oyster.' He pointed to the pearls and let out a maniacal laugh. 'Oyster! Ha! Ha! Ha! Ha!'

'You're mad!' accused Paparoa.

'Mad for power!' agreed Mayhem, cackling even more insanely. 'And those pearls will help me to get it.!'

He lurched off to help his men gather them up. When he reached an oyster bed, he gazed hungrily at the fortune that lay within it, then reached out with both hands.

The old priest had to fall back on a last line of

defence. Sneaking to a corner of the cave, he reached furtively into a moist hole in the side of the limestone rock. The conch shell which he brought out was much larger and whiter than the other.

'Wooooooooo!'

Paparoa blew a long shrill note on the conch.

The response was immediate. The oyster slammed shut and the VENOM agents were almost caught by the closing jaws. Miles Mayhem swung around in fury.

'What are you playing at, you old fool!'

'This is the Protector of the Cave,' explained Paparoa.

He held the conch shell to his lips again and blew.

'Woooooo!'

Mayhem charged towards him and grabbed the conch from his frail hands. Before the priest could stop him, he hurled the shell to the ground and stamped his heel on it. The conch was shattered into a dozen fragments.

Paparoa was stricken beyond belief.

'You've destroyed the Protector!'

'I'll destroy *you* if you try any more tricks,' said Mayhem.

'But the pearls have no defence now.'

As he spoke, the giant oysters opened once more to display the wealth that lay within. Miles Mayhem emitted another evil laugh.

'They're ours!' he yelled. 'Grab them!'

SEVEN

As the lunatic laughter reverberated around the cave, the VENOM leader went back to the oysters to gloat. The pearls were priceless. They would make him rich beyond the dreams of avarice. The wealth would be an important step towards making him and his agents the undisputed rulers of the world.

Paparoa had no means of stopping the plunder now.

'Get away from there,' he pleaded.

'Not a chance, old man.'

'I won't *let* you steal them.'

Summoning up all his wasted strength, the priest grabbed Mayhem by the arm and tried to drag him away. But he was no match for the big man. Mayhem

simply shrugged his shoulders and sent Paparoa hurtling across the cave.

'Now scram before I really lose my temper!'

'Aaaaaagh!'

The old man's scream sounded like a death-rattle.
As he stumbled backwards, he fell off the bank and
into the river. The strong current took a grip on him
and carried him away as if he were no more than a
splinter of wood.

'Get me out of here!' he cried.

Miles Mayhem peered into the water and smirked.

'Bon voyage!'

'Send us a postcard!' called Rax.

'That's got *him* out of the way!' said Malloy.

'Nothing can stop us now,' concluded Mayhem.

He picked up one of the great pearls and fondled it.
World power was at last within his grasp.

VENOM would triumph over MASK.

The canoe was making slow progress through the
water. They paddled hard but they were against the
current and it made their arms ache. Overhead, the
glow-worms provided a soft, pulsing light to guide
them.

'I wish we could go faster,' said Te Kaha.

'We'll get there,' promised Scott, increasing his
efforts.

'Thank you!'

T-Bob gazed up ahead and made some mirthful
noises.

'Now, there's a funny thing.'

'What is, T-Bob?' asked Scott.

'I never knew that fish had beards.'

'They don't *have* beards.'

'Well, *that* one does,' argued the robot. 'See? He's swimming towards us.'

Te Kaha looked in the direction indicated and she screamed.

'Eeeeee! It's grandfather!'

'I didn't know your grandad was a fish,' said T-Bob.

'He's being swept away,' she cried. 'He'll drown!'

'Not while I'm around!' promised Scott.

'Help!' gurgled Paparoa as he approached them.

'Catch hold of this!' shouted the boy.

He stuck out his paddle at just the right time. The priest was able to get a firm grip and they were able to pull him towards them. Once they had dragged him aboard, they paddled the canoe to the bank and secured the mooring rope to a jagged rock. While T-Bob steadied the craft, the children clambered out and helped the exhausted Paparoa ashore.

The old man lay on the ground with his head cradled by his loving granddaughter. It was minutes before he got enough breath back to tell them what had happened.

'Oh, my child!' he exclaimed. 'It's not safe to be here.'

'Why not, grandfather?'

'I have lost the Protector of the Cave and its secrets to some wicked men.'

'We know all about them,' she said.

'What's the Protector of the Cave?' asked Scott.

Paparoa eyed the stranger with grave suspicion.

'You can talk freely in front of Scott,' urged Te Kaha. 'He's a good friend. He's here with his father, Matt Trakker.'

'The kind man who has given all that money to safeguard our tribal heritage?' said the priest.

'That's my Dad,' replied Scott.

'Welcome to Glow-worm Grotto, my young friend.'

The boy shook hands with the old man then pressed for details of what Mayhem and his cohorts had actually done.

'There is a secret cave of giant pearls,' explained the priest. 'It is protected by a conch shell. One note from it and the oysters will close . . . but they destroyed the conch. There is no way to save the pearls now.'

'There *might* be,' murmured Scott.

'How?' asked Te Kaha.

'I'll show you . . . T-Bob, come over here!'

'*I* can't make the sound of a conch shell!' protested the robot with dignity. 'Nobody's going to blow into me.'

'I simply want to use the radio,' said Scott.

The boy flicked a few switches on the front panel of his metal companion and there was a burst of static. Scott bent in close to speak into the microphone.

'It's Scott! Can you hear me? It's Scott!'

He flicked a switch and the static increased.

'The cave is interfering with the radio signals.'

83

'Try again,' suggested Te Kaha.

'Yes, what about this switch?' added T-Bob.

He adjusted another switch and a blast of pop music filled the air. He giggled with embarrassment and switched it off.

'Sorry. Wrong station.'

The boy took charge once more and spoke urgently.

'Scott to MASK! Come in please! This is an emergency!'

The MASK vehicles were making their way through the grotto by courtesy of the glow-worms who formed a runway overhead. Inside Thunder Hawk, Matt and Bruce heard something on the radio but they could not make it out. They turned up the volume.

A familiar voice suddenly leapt out at them.

'Scott to MASK! Are you there, Dad?'

'Receiving you loud and clear, son,' replied Matt.

'That's great!'

'Are you safe?'

'*We* are but the pearls aren't!' said the boy.

'What pearls?'

'In the secret cave. That's what Te Kaha's grandfather was guarding. Giant pearls. Worth a fortune each. There's a sound you can make to close up the oysters. It's the noise of a conch shell.' Scott gulped for air after gabbling it all out. 'Can you help, Dad. VENOM are helping themselves to those pearls.'

'Leave it to us, son,' reassured Matt. 'Just get out of the cave with the others.'

He switched off the radio and his mask automatically dropped down over his head. Matt now punched various buttons on the console in front of him.

'I'll just have to try every frequency until I hit it,' he said. 'Spectrum, conch shell frequency scanner – on!'

His mask began to scan and emit a series of noises that were exactly like those from a conch shell. They varied in pitch and volume. Spectrum was getting close.

Back in the secret cave, Mayhem and his men heard the shrill notes echoing through the grotto. They had been harvesting the pearls and had put them in a large pile. They now paused to listen.

'What's that?' snarled Mayhem. 'I got rid of the Protector.'

'Woooooo!'

Spectrum had hit the right note at last. The sound produced the desired result. All the oysters closed with a bang. Sly Rax was pinched hard in the seat of his trousers and Mayhem himself was trapped inside an oyster for a few seconds. He forced his way out and scowled darkly.

'Who made them shut like that?' he howled.

Four vehicles came into the secret cave and stopped.

'I might have known!' said Mayhem. 'MASK.'

He turned to his men and barked his commands.

'Load those pearls into your sub, Rax! Malloy, get that bird of yours flying!'

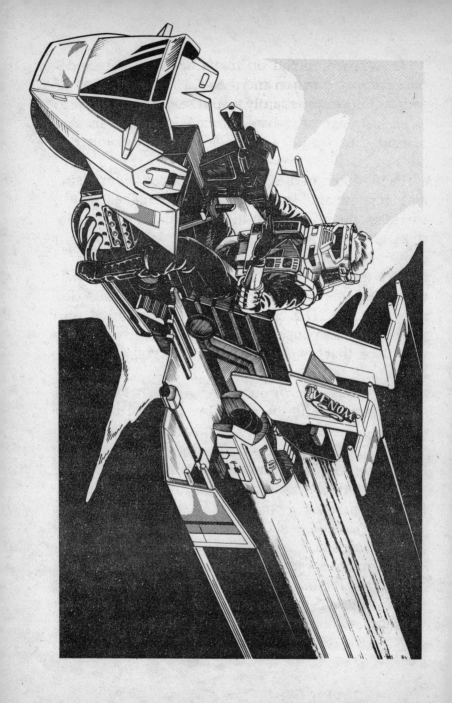

As Malloy jumped on to Vampire, his mask descended into position and the vehicle converted to air mode. It took off instantly before Mayhem had time to climb aboard. He waved his fist after the departing Malloy.

'You idiot! Come back!'

Firefly converted to jet mode and took off as well.

'I'm going after that scavenger!' asserted Julio.

He fired laser shots at the rear of Vampire but the cycle-jet swung round and fired back. A dogfight developed high up in the roof of the cave.

Rax, meanwhile, had loaded armfuls of pearls into Piranha. He climbed into it and his mask descended automatically. The vehicle sped away but Shark and Gator were blocking its path in the water.

Pulling a lever, Rax shot a torpedo at them. But Dusty and Gloria were too elusive. They manoeuvred their vehicles expertly out of the way. Dusty could not resist a mocking jeer.

'Close, Rax. But not close enough, fish bait!'

The torpedo exploded against a wall and brought tonnes of limestone tumbling down to block the exit that Rax was hoping to take. Piranha had to veer away and found itself on Shark's tail. Before Rax could fire at Gloria, she jettisoned a cloud of black ink into the water behind her. Piranha was completely disoriented.

The VENOM vehicle went round in a circle and created a huge wave just as Scott, Te Kaha, T-Bob and Paparoa came running into the cave to see what was

going on. The wave swept them straight into the river. Bruce Sato came to their rescue in a flash.

'Lifter – on!' he ordered.

All four of them were hit by the Lifter beam that shot out from his mask. They were taken clear of the water and deposited safely back on the bank.

'You okay?' asked Matt with concern.

'We're fine, Dad,' said Scott. 'Get back in action.'

Matt turned to continue his duel with Miles Mayhem.

Julio Lopez was still pursuing Malloy overhead, exchanging laser fire with him. Seeing the children on the bank below, Malloy fired a cannonade of buckshot out of the rear of his vehicle. The buckshot dislodged a series of large stalactites which dropped down like huge knives. Scott and the others were able to dodge them without difficulty.

Julio was annoyed at the attack on unarmed children.

'Take this, Vampire!' he yelled.

His mask sent a series of energy hoops shooting through the air until they imprisoned Vampire. The VENOM vehicle had no control over its movements. It sped on and collided with the largest stalactite of all, burying itself in the limestone before falling to the ground with a deafening thud.

Rax was still trying to make his escape but Gloria Baker had him in her sights. She fired a magnetic harpoon at Piranha. It lodged itself in the vehicle's rear, then exploded. Rax and the pearls were sent

flying high into the air. They landed in one of the oysters which was obligingly open. Battered and bruised, Rax sat there with armfuls of pearls.

The MASK team could not help laughing.

Matt Trakker, meanwhile, had been fighting it out with Miles Mayhem. The men stood some distance apart and used their masks to fire at each other. When Mayhem saw that his henchmen had been brought down, he conceded defeat and took to his heels.

'I'm getting out of this grotto!' he yelled.

He used Viper to burn a hole in the limestone rock then made good his escape. A minute later, he was beating a hasty retreat in Switchblade. Without any of the giant pearls.

'I'll get you for this, MASK!' he howled.

But once again he had been put to flight by Matt Trakker and his agents. The Maori treasure had been saved.

Everyone joined in the celebrations back at the village. Matt, Scott, T-Bob, Te Kaha, Paparoa, Dusty, Bruce, Julio and Gloria sat at the low table with Chief Kaitaia. The Maori leader thanked his friends again and again for all they had done.

Te Kaha singled out Scott for a special mention.

'He was magnificent,' she said.

Once again, she rubbed her nose gently against his. Scott went redder than ever and the adults smiled. The girl did not forget how much T-Bob had helped. She turned to thank him in the same way.

'Not again!' said the robot. 'This nose is not for rubbing!'

He jumped up and backed quickly away from her.

T-Bob had survived all the perils inside the cave but the attentions of the beautiful Maori girl were too much for his circuits to handle. He could not turn red and so he bounced up and down instead.

The whole village shook with happy laughter.

If you have enjoyed The Plunder of Glow-Worm Grotto, stand by for . . .

MASK 7 – THE EVERGLADES ODDITY

The MASK mission is to rescue a Space Shuttle from the clutches of VENOM. When Matt Trakker is laid low, Scott and T-Bob lend a hand in a very dangerous assignment.

MASK 8 – DRAGONFIRE

The MASK mission this time is to protect the Temple of the Dragons from the vile atrocities of the VENOM agents. Scott and T-Bob find themselves again at the forefront of an adventure – in an exotic part of the world.

COMING SOON!

KNIGHT BOOKS

Six stunning MASK adventures from Knight Books

☐	39890 6	MASK 1 – The Deathstone	£1.95
☐	39891 4	MASK 2 – Peril Under Paris	£1.95
☐	39892 2	MASK 3 – Venice Menace	£1.95
☐	39977 5	MASK 4 – Book of Power	£1.95
☐	40327 6	MASK 5 – Panda Power	£1.95
☐	41535 5	MASK 6 – The Plunder of Glow-worm Grotto	£1.95

All these books are available at your local bookshop or newsagent, or can be ordered direct from the publisher. Just tick the titles you want and fill in the form below.

Prices and availability subject to change without notice.

Knight Books, P.O. Box 11, Falmouth TR10 9EN, Cornwall.

Please send cheque or postal order, and allow the following for postage and packing:

U.K. – 55p for one book, plus 22p for the second book, and 14p for each additional book ordered up to a £1.75 maximum.

B.F.P.O. and EIRE – 55p for the first book, plus 22p for the second book, and 14p per copy for the next 7 books, 8p per book thereafter.

OTHER OVERSEAS CUSTOMERS – £1.00 for the first book, plus 25p per copy for each additional book.

Please send cheque or postal order (no currency).

Name ....

Address ....

....